This book should be returned to any branch of the
Lancashire County Library on or before the date shown

30 APR 2018

21 MAR 2020

Lancashire County Library
Bowran Street
Preston PR1 2UX
www.lancashire.gov.uk/libraries

Lancashire
County
Council

LL1(A)

Collect all of Rascal's adventures:

Rascal

FACING THE FLAMES

CHRIS COOPER

ILLUSTRATED BY JAMES DE LA RUE

EGMONT

EGMONT

We bring stories to life

First published as *Tramp: Facing the Flames* by Puffin in 2003
This edition first published in Great Britain in 2015
by Egmont UK Limited
The Yellow Building, 1 Nicholas Road, London W11 4AN

Text copyright © 2003 Chris Cooper
Illustration copyright © 2015 James de la Rue
The moral rights of the author and illustrator have been asserted

ISBN: 978 1 4052 7531 6

58627/1

www.egmont.co.uk

A CIP catalogue record for this title is available from the British Library

Typeset by Avon DataSet Ltd, Bidford on Avon, Warwickshire
Printed and bound in Great Britain by CPI Group

MIX
Paper
FSC FSC® C018306

For Uncle Leonard and Aunt Sandy

CHAPTER 1

The sun had passed its noontime high point in the sky, but it still beat down fiercely. The shade of the forest offered Rascal little protection from its heat. Even the strong wind was hot and dry and gave no relief from the sun's rays.

More than anything in the world, Rascal wanted water right now – a long, cool drink of delicious water. He was hungry too, of course, but he could get along without food for now – he'd had a lot of practice at that recently, after all. But no living thing could survive long without water. If he didn't get a drink soon, he would be unable to take another step.

Many dogs would have stopped already; stopped and just lain down in the shade until the cool of the evening arrived. But Rascal would not give up. Whenever he felt as if he couldn't go on, the thought of who waited for him at journey's end spurred him on. Joel! It was the thought of his master, Joel, that had kept Rascal going for the hundreds of miles he had travelled so far. And it was the thought of Joel that would keep him going for the many miles that lay ahead too.

Now, if he could just find a drink of water . . .

He wasn't the only one thinking this way. It seemed that the whole forest around him was also crying out for water. It had struggled for too long without a drop of rain in this scorching summer. For days Rascal had thought that the drought would end, but somehow he always seemed to run ahead of the bank of clouds to the east.

The evidence of the dry season was all around Rascal in the pale colours of the foliage. The lower branches of the trees were a dusty grey and the grasses and brush were more a washed-out yellow than a healthy green. Shrivelled brown leaves crackled beneath the dog's feet and brittle pine needles dug into the pads on his paws.

As he neared the ridge that ran along the top of this hill, he heard a sound above the noise of the wind. It was human voices, laughing. He could also hear the low crackle of a campfire and the smell of roasted meat.

Soon Rascal could see four people – two women and two men, all in their early twenties – sitting outside their badly pitched tents, which flapped precariously in the wind. One of the men was prodding a long stick into the

campfire. Several objects wrapped in tinfoil sat in the fire.

'Don't think these potatoes are done yet,' said the man.

No one seemed to mind. They were all finishing off hamburgers which had also been cooked on this fire (judging from the charred smell).

'Shouldn't we just have had something cold to eat?' said the woman with short red hair. 'I mean, it's hot enough already without having to light a fire.'

The man with the stick grinned. 'Listen, Debs. It isn't proper camping if you don't build a fire, is it?'

The other man, who had a scrubby beard, took a drink from a silver can and laughed. 'We never knew you were such a Boy Scout, Rick.'

The man called Rick did a silly salute with his free hand. 'Didn't you see me start this fire by rubbing two sticks together?'

'Course we did,' laughed the other woman, whose fair hair was pulled back into a ponytail. 'But I bet those matches in your pocket came in handy too!'

Rascal listened to them talking and joking for a few minutes more. He was waiting for clues, anything that might tell him if these people were the sort who would be kind to a stray dog like himself. His long, hard journey had taught Rascal this about the behaviour of humans – some of them were wonderful and some of them were terrible, and many times you couldn't tell which was which until it was too late.

But his thirst wouldn't let him delay any longer. Rascal stood and pushed his way through the undergrowth towards the four people.

'Hey, look!' said the woman called Debs. 'It's a dog!'

'He could probably smell those

burgers,' said the man with the beard. 'He must like *his* food burnt to a crisp as well!'

'He does look hungry,' said the second woman. 'Shall we give him something to eat?'

'No chance!' exclaimed Rick. 'If he

wants a burger, he can go and buy his own, can't he?' He was holding the end of his stick in the heart of the campfire. After a few seconds he pulled it out, a flame now burning at the end. He waved it in Rascal's direction as if it were a sword. 'Clear off, wild beast!' he shouted, making his voice boom.

Rascal was tensed to run, but he could tell that the man was not really threatening him so much as trying to make his friends laugh.

'I don't think he reckons much to your flaming torch, Rick,' said Debs. She was opening the top of a big plastic bottle of water. She poured a splash out to wash her hands.

Rascal couldn't help himself. When he saw that water he let out a little yap.

'Hold on, I don't think it *is* burgers he's after,' commented the woman with the ponytail. 'Look at him eyeing up that water. He wants a drink.'

'Can't blame him, in this heat,' said Debs. She poured some of the water into a plastic bowl and handed it to the man with the beard. 'Poor thing . . . Go on, give this to him.'

'Me? What if he's got rabies or something?' complained the man. But he took the bowl and stood up.

Rascal watched his every step as he came closer.

The man took a drag on his cigarette and looked back at his friends. 'Tell you what,' he smirked. 'I'll give him a drink, but first he's got to do a few tricks. Fair enough?'

He turned back to the dog and held out a hand. 'Shake paws,' he said.

Rascal watched that hand as if it were a cat in a tree, but he didn't lift a paw.

'Don't be so mean!' yelled the ponytailed woman. 'He hasn't got a clue what you're on about.'

But this wasn't true. Back in the old days when he was with his master, Joel, Rascal had seen other dogs in the local park do little tricks like this. Their masters would give some order or other and then the dog would shake paws or sit up and beg, or something like that. He even remembered one dog, a wire-haired terrier, that would 'dance' on command, jumping up and letting its master hold its front paws while it hopped around on the back two. On a different command, the dog would whirl round and round, breathlessly chasing its tail.

A lot of people in the park had laughed, but not Rascal's master. When he'd seen the terrier, Joel had ruffled his own dog's ears and whispered, 'Don't worry, boy, I won't ever make you do stupid tricks like that!'

But now, in the afternoon heat of the forest, many miles from everyone he knew and everything he loved, Rascal watched this bearded man commanding him to do one of those same stupid tricks.

The dog sat as still as stone.

The man glanced back quickly at his friends. 'OK then, we'll try something else.' He flicked his cigarette butt away. Then he bent down and patted the dusty earth with the flat of his hand. 'Roll over and die!' he commanded. 'Come on! Roll over and die!'

Rascal wasn't sure what this meant, but it didn't matter. He wasn't going to perform tricks for the entertainment of these people.

He threw a glance at the water in the bowl. It looked wonderful, but he knew in his heart that he wouldn't get a drop of it. He ducked his head down and edged forwards, just to make sure. The man jerked the bowl back – 'Not yet!

Wait for it!' – and sloshed water on to the dry ground.

Rascal didn't need to see any more. He gave a single bark of defiance and began to trot away.

'Hey,' the man was saying. 'Don't you *want* a drink then?'

But Rascal didn't even look back, and soon the laughing voices of the four people were lost in the howl of the wind.

CHAPTER 2

It became harder and harder to carry on down the hill that sloped away from the ridge. Rascal's whole body was aching, but worst of all was his parched and cracked throat. He didn't dare try to swallow. Rascal hardly noticed when a

flock of birds raced westward overhead,
cawing in noisy alarm. He couldn't keep
his mind on anything but the thought of
water.

But then the undergrowth around
him began to look a little greener, not
so dry and brittle. As he pushed his way
through the long grass and bushes, fewer
stalks snapped off. Instead they were

bending as he passed and then springing
back. It could mean only one thing . . .
Rascal forced himself to speed up.

He heard it first, the wonderful sound
of running water. A few more metres
and then he was looking at it. A stream!

It wasn't very big – from the dry

patches on either side it was clear that many rainless days had shrunk it. But it was enough! Rascal launched himself into the flowing water.

It wasn't very deep either, and the dog was able to wade right into it. The cold made his legs ache, but this wasn't bad — it was a *good* ache because it carried the promise of a refreshing drink ahead.

He hesitated for a second, enjoying the idea of what was to come. Then Rascal dipped his head and began to lap up water with his parched tongue. It tasted better than anything he'd ever known. EVER! He slurped the water eagerly, not caring that it splashed all over his face or that his ears dipped into it. And as he drank and drank, he felt the strength returning to his body. His tiredness did not disappear altogether – that would take more than a drink of water, he'd need a big bowl of food and a good night's sleep for that – but it faded to a tolerable level.

The dog was once again able to think about things other than his own terrible thirst, was able to pay attention to his surroundings again. It was then that Rascal heard another human voice a little further down the stream and around a bend.

'TELL HIM TO STOP IT, MUM!'

It was a young girl's voice and it was high with frustration.

A woman's voice came in reply. She sounded distracted.

'Leave your sister be, Kevin, and stop teasing! I won't tell you again.'

Rascal's first thought was simply to move on. He'd already had one bad experience with humans today. He didn't want another so soon. But he was so comfortable there in the cool of the water that he listened a moment longer.

'I was just trying to help her get across,' said an older boy's voice, obviously making an effort to sound as innocent as he could. 'It's not my fault she's scared of everything!'

'Kevin . . .' warned a man's voice, then, more kindly, 'Do you need some help there, Hailey?'

'No!' answered the girl crossly. 'And I'm NOT scared!'

It wasn't exactly curiosity that made Rascal move towards the curve in the stream. Although bitter experience had shown him that it wasn't always there, a deep part of him was still ready to look for the goodness in people.

As he rounded the bend, Rascal saw a family of four further down the stream. The two adults were bent over their smartphones, trying to get reception to make their maps work. A backpack lay on the grass next to them. The woman pushed a strand of hair off her face and shook the phone impatiently, trying to get the map to load. The man was staring at his own phone in frustration.

Meanwhile, the children were playing in the stream. A young girl stood with

both feet on a rock in the middle of the
water. She had apparently crossed the
three stepping stones behind her, but the
final jump to dry land was the biggest.

Her brother was watching from the
bank, unimpressed.

'Go on then,' he challenged, arms

folded. 'You can't always be the world-champion chicken!'

The young girl's face creased in determination. She bent her legs, getting ready to leap, but she didn't do it. She couldn't. It was as if her legs wouldn't obey her.

Finally her dad looked up and noticed that she still hadn't made it across the stream. He sighed and placed his useless phone carefully on the grass, then went over to the bank.

'Come on, Hailey,' he said. He pulled his trainers off and stepped into the moving water. 'It really isn't very deep,' he sighed. 'The worst that would happen is that you'd get a bit wet.' He carried his daughter to the bank. 'Now just give us a minute, you two, will you?' he went on. 'Your mother and I need to check something,' He returned to his phone, carrying his trainers with him.

Rascal watched as the older boy glanced back at his parents, who were once again staring at their phones as if mentally willing them to reveal the right way to go. The boy grinned and muttered, 'The world champion!' Then he made a low noise, clearly intended to sound like a chicken: '*Bwaak-buk-bukka!*'

The girl didn't answer, but stared at her brother furiously. The boy said something else; Rascal couldn't hear what it was over the sound of the wind. And then suddenly the girl whirled around and ran away through the trees.

At first her brother just watched in silent disbelief, the triumphant grin frozen on his face. Then he said, 'Er . . .'

'What is it NOW?' began his mum. 'We just –' Then she looked up. 'Hailey?'

'Where's your sister?' demanded his dad.

The grin had fled from the boy's face now. 'She just went off into the woods.' He pointed a finger helplessly. 'That way.'

His dad had pulled his trainers back on and was running towards the trees.

'Hailey!' he shouted, but there was no reply.

'HAILEY!' he shouted again, louder this time and with panic growing in his voice. But the wind just threw his words back at him.

He turned to the other two – 'You wait here, OK?' – and then he plunged into the woods.

CHAPTER 3

The girl had gone east, in the direction
Rascal had come from. It was the wrong
route for the dog – his final destination
lay west – but he knew that he couldn't
leave without helping. There was no
way of knowing if the man would be

able to find the small child in the tangle
of trees and bushes, especially with the
wind roaring and drowning out all
voices. Besides, Rascal knew how useless
humans were at finding others – it was
almost as if they had no noses at all!

He could hear the mother saying,
'What did you say to her, Kevin?'

'Nothing,' answered the boy in a
wounded tone.

Neither of them had noticed the dog.
Before they did, Rascal left the cool of
the stream – now he too ran back eastwards
into the forest. He could hear the girl's
father shouting, but his voice was faint.

As he sniffed deeply, Rascal caught the
faintest trace of the girl – and *not* in the
direction her father was heading.

But there was a problem. Usually it
would have been simple for Rascal to
find the child. His nose would have led
him straight to her, nothing to it. But he
was suddenly aware of an acrid smell of
smoke. It wasn't very strong, but it still

cloaked almost every other scent.

Rascal realised that this had been in the air for some time, but he just hadn't paid attention to it. It was only a fire, after all, and fire was something he had always associated with humans. They knew how to handle it, didn't they? In the good old days, when he'd lived with Joel, he'd seen people make huge fires, with crowds gathering round them in some sort of celebration and no one seeming the least bit worried.

And yet . . . Although the domesticated, 'pet' side of him wasn't worried, the deeper animal part of his brain recognised the danger. *Fire can spiral out of control*, it whispered, *fast* . . .

Nevertheless, Rascal forced himself to go on, moving slowly and trying to pick out the girl's scent in the middle of the smoky smell, which seemed to be getting stronger and stronger.

Suddenly something burst out of the trees ahead, charging right towards him. It wasn't the girl or her father. It was a fox.

Rascal tensed himself, but the wild animal didn't seem to notice the dog. Its eyes were wide with fear. It was running away from something, something that had terrified it. But nothing else crashed through the undergrowth in pursuit.

Rascal watched in confusion as the fox disappeared into the bushes behind him and raced towards the stream.

The acrid smell was getting worse now, and the wind was blowing it straight down towards him. His eyes began to sting. Rascal looked up and saw smoke rising above the trees ahead.

He was aware of a distant roaring that seemed somehow different from that of the wind. A terrible thought surfaced in Rascal's mind. *What if this was a fire that humans DIDN'T have under control?*

He padded forwards nervously. There was a thin haze of smoke all around him now.

It was impossible for him to smell
anything else and it was just chance that
allowed him to spot a glimpse of the
girl's blue T-shirt.

She was sitting with her back to a tree.
Her face was pressed into her knees, her
hands by her temples.

Rascal approached carefully, not
wanting to alarm the young girl. When
he was just a couple of metres away,
Hailey looked up. Tear tracks glistened
on her cheeks.

'Mummy?' she said. 'Daddy?'

When she saw that it was a dog, she
pressed her back into the tree nervously.

Rascal moved towards her, taking care not to scare the girl any more. He pushed his snout closer and licked her hand. After a moment's hesitation, she flung her arm around him and pressed her face into the fur on his neck.

At first there was nothing but tears. Finally she found words, throwing them out between sobbing gasps. 'I . . . wanted . . . to . . . to show him . . . I'm not . . . not scared,' she managed.

Rascal understood that the only thing he could do for now was sit here and wait. The girl didn't appear to have noticed the haze of smoke clouding the air like morning mist.

The wind died down for an instant and Rascal heard a strange noise from up the hill. There was a series of pops – they sounded a bit like the fireworks Joel and his family set off once a year – and a kind of crackling roar. Rascal's nerves were screaming at him now. He could no longer pretend that everything was OK, that the humans had everything under control.

'What was that?' asked Hailey in alarm, looking back.

Rascal gave a little bark. He didn't want to frighten the girl more, but she had to get moving. When she didn't, Rascal threw back his head and barked louder, hoping that the girl's father would hear him and understand that his daughter was here too. But the wind had picked up again. There was little chance of being heard.

He looked back at Hailey. She couldn't be more than five or six years old. One thing was certain – he couldn't abandon her.

Suddenly there was a movement in the undergrowth behind Hailey. Another creature was heading in the direction of the stream. It was a snake and it was moving straight towards her.

CHAPTER 4

Hailey had her back turned to the rust-and-mud-coloured snake. She hadn't seen it.

Rascal watched as the reptile slithered closer to the girl, only its flat, wedge-shaped head off the ground. Though he

had never come across anything like it before, Rascal's animal instincts told him that this snake was dangerous. He was right – one bite from its venomous fangs would be deadly.

The dog's heart was beating fast, the blood was surging in his body and his legs were screaming at him to run away, yet Rascal would not give in to his instincts. He had to protect the girl, but there was no telling what she would do if she noticed the snake. If she let out a scream or made any kind of loud noise, the snake would surely strike at her. She didn't even have time to move quickly

out of the snake's way — it was already
too close for that. What could Rascal
do?

Suddenly he realised. He sensed
that the snake would not attack unless
provoked. The girl's best chance lay in
sitting completely still — that way the
snake would just make its way past
her. But the only possibility of that
happening would be if she wasn't even
aware of the reptile's presence until the
danger had passed.

Rascal had to focus the girl's attention
on something else. He might not be
a dog who performed silly tricks to

entertain people, but this was different.
He jumped up and began to spin round,
chasing his tail.

Hailey sat watching him with
a mixture of amusement and
bewilderment on her face. What on
earth was this silly dog doing? A small,
nervous laugh escaped her.

Rascal stopped whirling round and round. The snake had slithered past Hailey, who had stayed perfectly still as she watched the dog's antics.

Now Rascal had to make sure that the snake didn't get too close to *him*. But before he could move away to safety, Hailey spotted the reptile's reddish body. She let out a short cry of fear. The snake paused, its triangular head high up off the ground now, its slender tongue tasting the air.

Suddenly the snake flashed forwards, right at Rascal, who was still within striking distance. The dog had only an

instant to react. His legs were weary, but fear gave them enough strength for one mighty leap. The snake's fangs met only air.

But as Rascal landed, one of his back feet struck a rock and he tumbled over. Even before he had scrambled up to his feet, the snake was right next to him, mouth open and fangs at the ready.

Rascal looked fearfully at the deadly

reptile. But the snake made no attempt to strike a second time. Rascal was no longer in its path and so it continued on its way towards the stream and vanished into the undergrowth. Just like the fox before, it too was fleeing from something.

The snake had gone, but there was no time for any relief that the danger had passed. No, it became clear now why the animals had been been fleeing. The smoke was suddenly thicker – it had become much worse very quickly – and the searing wind blew ashes at dog and girl. They both looked up the hill. For

the first time Rascal saw a distant swirl
of flames, high up in the tops of the
trees.

Hailey was frozen in fear. She gazed
at the far-off flames and the billowing
smoke as if she couldn't quite believe
they were real. Rascal too stared at the
fire, his mind in a fog of confusion and
disbelief.

Then a pine tree suddenly exploded
with a sound like an immense
firecracker as the resin in it overheated.
A chunk of burning wood was hurled to
the next tree, and another to the next. In
this way, the fire was advancing rapidly

towards them.

Rascal finally kicked into action. He nudged his snout into the girl's side and got her moving down the hill, back towards the stream. At first, panic made her run too fast. She couldn't see where she was going and her foot caught on a tree root, making her tumble forwards. After that, Rascal ran in front of her, trying to make sure she didn't fall again.

The smoke hurt Rascal's lungs as he ran. The girl's rasping cough told him that she was suffering too. It felt as if they had been running for ever. Had they gone in the wrong direction? With

all this smoke in the forest, it was easy to become disorientated.

But then Rascal recognised where they were. The stream wasn't too far ahead of them now.

From up the hill behind them, the fire roared like distant thunder that never ended.

CHAPTER 5

Minutes later, dog and girl had
positioned themselves in the middle
of the stream, not far from the row of
stepping stones where Rascal had first
seen Hailey and her family.

Rascal instinctively felt that they

should stay near the water. They would be safe here, wouldn't they? In a way, it didn't matter – Hailey had flopped into the water, gasping for breath. He wasn't sure she would be able to go on.

They weren't the only ones in the forest who had sought safety in the gently running waters. A little further down the stream, Rascal saw the fox, half-running and half-swimming. A

family of possums huddled at the edge of the water, their voices a thin chorus of frightened squeaks.

But there was no sign of Hailey's family.

Rascal looked nervously at the girl. Her eyes were red and watering. Was it because of the stinging smoke that continued to pour down the slope from the east, or something else? But then –

'They're not here!' cried the girl. 'I want my mummy and daddy!'

There was nothing Rascal could do but press closer against her. His legs and belly still felt cool in the water, but the

air above the
surface of
the water
was getting
hotter and
hotter as the
wind swept
down the hill. It
roared and beat at them like
a living thing.

'They'll be back here any minute,'
Hailey was saying, though her trembling
voice betrayed her true feelings. 'They'll
be right back, I know they will.'

The smoke around them continued to

thicken. When Rascal looked up, he was
unable to see any more than a thin slice
of blue sky. Billowing smoke covered
the rest, as huge and threatening as
thunderclouds.

Despite the darkening smoke, they
could see no more flames as they looked
back up the slope to the east. They had
managed
to outrun
the fire
down the
hill. Perhaps
it would just
burn itself out.

Most forest fires did, after all. Perhaps it wouldn't even reach the stream.

But soon the smoke was dotted with burning embers. They glowed orange and red in the dim light. A few of them landed in the stream with an angry hissing noise. Minutes later, flames became visible to the east. It looked like a wall of fire, making its way down the slope and devouring everything in its path. It seemed to be moving much faster now, blown on by the fierce wind. Its endless roar was punctuated by popping noises as air pockets ignited in the trees.

The air was becoming so hot it was hard to breathe. Would the stream continue to keep them safe? Rascal bent down to duck his head under the water. Was the surface lower now? It seemed so, and a layer of ashes lay on top.

Panic swept through Rascal. He ran quickly to the bend in the stream.

'Wait!' cried Hailey in alarm. 'Where are you go—'

But Rascal had reached the bend and could now see what was happening further upstream. The forest fire had moved even faster there. It had reached the stream, but the water wasn't stopping it. The treetops were bent by the strength of the wind and the fire was jumping across to the other side.

The air there was a whirlwind of embers and ashes. It was clear that the stream, which looked weaker and smaller by the minute, could offer no protection.

The same would be true when the fire reached their stretch of the water. They would have to keep going, that's all there was to it. But where? The forest immediately to the west here was too dense — it would take them too long to fight their way through. They would have to follow the stream.

Rascal splashed back to Hailey and began to bark frantically, hoping that she would understand. He ran past her and paused, looking back over his shoulder.

'I–I–I can't go,' stammered the girl, eyes wide with terror. 'My mum and dad, they'll probably come back here, they . . .'

Rascal barked again. It didn't have much effect on the girl, but at that moment another pine tree erupted into flames, blasting a burning branch towards the stream. It fell just short of the water and immediately began to

burn up the long grass there, crackling and spitting as it charred the earth.

Hailey didn't say anything. She just nodded, and then the two of them were making their way downstream, wading through the shallow water as fast as they could.

CHAPTER 6

Soon the fire was nearing the creek, catching up to them. But the woods to their right were a little clearer now, so they would be able to head west. The noise was terrible. For just an instant, Rascal thought he heard a different sound inside the din of the fire, a distant voice shouting somewhere beyond the fire to their left.

He paused, trying to identify exactly where it had come from. Then it vanished as a new sound grew gradually louder and louder – *shup, shup, shup.*

'A helicopter!' cried Hailey.

They both stared up, but they were unable to see anything through the smoke above them. The noise of the helicopter

held constant for a few minutes. Was it rescuing someone? The person who had cried out? There was no way of knowing, and there was no way of getting beyond the fire line to find out.

Then the noise of the helicopter began to subside.

'Come back!' shouted Hailey, but it was no good. Soon there was nothing but the roar of the fire. They were on their own.

Rascal and Hailey left the stream behind them and ran west, where the land began to climb again. The hot wind pushed at their backs. The smoke and embers were a continuous reminder that the fire was close behind them.

By now Hailey was panting hard. They had run a long way, but, to make things worse, every breath they took seared their lungs and made them want to cough and cough.

The girl was slowing down. She couldn't help it. Finally, she stopped, bending forwards with her hands on her knees. Unable to speak, she tried desperately to suck in some air that wasn't thick with smoke.

Rascal stopped too. Hope had begun to lift his spirit. After all, if they had managed to outrun the fire down the slope on the other side of the stream, surely they could outrun it now uphill?

There was one thing that Rascal didn't know, however — a forest fire is one of the few things in the world that moves faster uphill than it can downhill. When the dog looked back towards the stream, he was shocked at how quickly the blaze had followed them. It had crossed the stream, leaping over the treetops.

Hailey had seen it too. Her face was twisted in pain and fear, one hand clutched at the stitch in her side, but she began to run again.

A few minutes later, they came across a dirt path through the trees. It was much easier to run on this than it was to battle their way through the bushes and undergrowth of the forest. Maybe they would get away safely . . . The fire crackled and roared behind them, a constant reminder of what the alternative was.

Then suddenly there was a break in the trees. The path widened into a viewing area. A low fence with a small warning sign next to it curved around the far side of the open ground.

Rascal edged closer. Beyond the fence,

the ground
fell away
to nothing
in front of
him. It was
a drop of over
two metres.

There was no way
they could climb down. They were
going to have to jump. Rascal waited for
Hailey. When she reached the edge, her
eyes widened at the sight of the drop.

Finally she gave a tearful nod.
She stepped over the fence and helped
Rascal do the same.

'One, two . . . THREE!'

On the girl's final word, Rascal understood that they were to jump together. He bounded forwards, clear of a boulder below, and landed in a heap.

But where was Hailey?

Rascal looked back. The girl hadn't jumped. She was still there at the edge, tensed to jump but unmoving. The dog realised that he'd seen her exactly like this before, when she had been trying to jump from the stepping stone to the bank of the stream.

Hailey's lips were moving. She was mumbling something but Rascal

couldn't make out the words, not
with the noise of the blaze, which was
approaching fast behind her.

Then Hailey's voice got louder and
stronger, saying the same thing over and
over again until she was shouting it.

'I . . . AM . . . NOT . . .'

She yelled out the final word in mid-
air as she jumped forwards with arms
aloft.

'SCARED!'

She landed on both feet and fell
forwards into the dusty ground. For a
moment, she remained on hands and
knees, trying to get her breath back.
Then she looked up at Rascal. Her face
was grimy and her eyes were still wide
with fear. But she gave the dog a flicker
of a smile.

The smile vanished as soon as she

stood. Her left ankle immediately gave way. When she straightened again, it was clear that she was in a lot of pain. She couldn't put much weight on the foot at all and had to limp forwards, wincing every time she put pressure on the injured ankle.

Rascal spotted a fair-sized stick to

the side of the path. He picked it up with his teeth and carried it to Hailey. The girl understood right away. She took hold of it and began using it as a walking stick. As she got used to it, they managed to pick up a little speed. They had to — the break in the forest behind them would slow the fire down but not stop it.

As they carried on, the land began to level off and the trees thinned out. Rascal was aware of a different kind of noise up ahead of them — the whine of some sort of machinery. That meant people, and people meant safety! Hope fluttered in his heart.

But when they rounded a corner a terrible sight confronted them. The fire was straight ahead!

CHAPTER 7

Rascal was lost in confusion. How was
this possible? Had they taken a wrong
turning? Had he somehow guided them
back towards the fire? He looked behind
them. No, judging from the billowing
smoke, there must be flames still raging

up the side of the hill. What was going on? Had the blaze run ahead of them to the north and then somehow curved back around on itself, cutting them off?

Whatever the explanation, there was another smaller line of fire ahead of them. They were caught in a deadly trap with no escape! For just an instant, Rascal's bravery disappeared. He slumped to the ground, defeated. With flames all around, there was nowhere else to go.

But then Hailey was shouting to him, her voice strong.

'Look! There are people there!'

Rascal raised his head. It was true! Not far beyond the fire in front of them he could see several people wearing bright yellow clothing and blue hard hats.

'They're firefighters!' gasped Hailey. 'And Mummy and Daddy are with them, and Kevin, I *bet* they are! Come on!'

Through the shimmer of smoke and flames, Rascal could see only one of the firefighters properly. She was holding a kind of burning torch and she ran it across a line of brush. The next instant it burst into flames. The firefighters were setting a new fire themselves! By burning a backfire (a smaller fire set in the path of the main one), they hoped to deprive the main fire of fuel and oxygen. The machinery noise began again.

It was the sound of a chainsaw and it was followed seconds later by a crashing noise as a tree toppled. The firefighters were trying to create a gap that the forest fire could not jump.

Of course, Rascal didn't understand this. He didn't have to. He just knew that their only hope of survival lay with these people. Suddenly Hailey shouted, 'There's a gap! There's a gap in the fire!' She began hobbling towards a spot where the flames had died down. Rascal followed her. The ground was so hot, it felt as if the pads on his feet were blistering. His eyes were bloodshot and painfully sore from all the smoke.

As the girl and dog approached the gap, a few of the firefighters spotted them. There was a lot of urgent shouting. Within seconds, a blast of water had been turned on this section of the backfire to widen the gap. Another firefighter ran towards them.

'You're going to be OK,' he reassured Hailey.

She threw aside her stick and let
the firefighter pick her up and carry
her back to safety. As he did so, the
firefighter looked down at the dog
trotting wearily at his feet. Beneath his
helmet, the man's teeth looked bright in
his ash-covered face.

'You are one good dog,' he said.

A few firefighters continued to feed the backfire with their drip-torches. Behind the backfire, there was a whirlwind of different activities. Some people were hauling away branches cut down by the chainsaws. Further down the line, a small bulldozer was scooping up debris and shoving it to either side, carving a wide, bare path along the forest floor.

Rascal stuck with them as the firefighter took Hailey to a small yellow truck. A woman firefighter stood at the back of it, holding a walkie-talkie to her mouth.

'The planes are on their way,' she said, 'but it'll be a while yet. Is this –?'

'Her name's Hailey,' said the man. 'She wants to know if we've seen her m–'

Before he could finish, Hailey's mum burst out of the front of the truck. She rushed forwards and took her daughter into her arms.

'Hailey, you're safe, you're OK, he found you . . .' They hugged tightly and wept tears of relief.

Kevin was there too. He hung back, looking pale and stunned by the events of the afternoon.

Finally Hailey's mother looked up and around. A puzzled look settled on her face.

'Wh-where's your father?' she asked.

CHAPTER 8

'So here's the situation,' explained the
firefighter, the one who had led Rascal
and Hailey to safety. His name was
Mike and he was talking to the woman
with the radio. 'Hailey here got lost in
the woods and her dad went to look

for her. After a while he went back to the stream to see if she'd returned. She hadn't, but that's when the family saw the smoke. Hailey's mum and brother set off for safety right away.'

The woman, who was the firefighter's superior officer, turned to the family. Her expression was grim.

'But your husband stayed?' she asked Hailey's mum. 'He stayed to look for the girl?'

Hailey's mum just nodded and clutched her daughter's hand.

'The rangers have sent out a search team,' continued Mike. 'We've lost contact with them now but the last we heard they were north of the fire. The only people they came across were four campers who had managed to get over the ridge to the other side of the fire.'

'What about the helicopter?' asked the woman.

Mike shook his head grimly. 'It scanned the area but they couldn't see anything through the smoke.'

Rascal lay still as the talk went back and forth over his head. He knew from the urgent tone of the voices how serious this was.

Mike was pointing down at a map

spread out in the back of the truck. He indicated an area near the stream. 'This is where the Armstrong family was to begin with,' he said. 'OK, Hailey had to jump over the bluff, so she must have left the stream here.' He drew a line a little further down the map with his finger. 'Mr Armstrong would have stayed

on this side of the river until he found
Hailey, but the fire would have driven
him south. Because Hailey didn't see
him, I reckon that means he has to be
somewhere here.' He circled a wide area
on the map with his finger.

The officer bit her lower lip. 'Maybe,
but even if you're right, we can't spare
anyone else to go and check. We haven't
even got enough people to maintain the
backfire.'

But Mike wouldn't give up. 'I can go
alone,' he said, pointing at the map. 'The
fire hasn't moved very far south yet. I
can loop south, cross the stream and

then come round under the front line of the fire. If he's there, I'll find him.'

There were several seconds of silence. Finally the officer nodded agreement. Rascal watched as Mike ran off and swept up a large backpack of equipment. The dog understood immediately – the man was going out into the fire. He was going to try to find Hailey's dad.

Rascal didn't hesitate. He slipped out from under Kevin's hand and raced after the firefighter.

Mike was already running towards the flames when he noticed the dog at his heels.

'Do you know where I'm going?' he asked.

A single bark was the answer.

Mike grinned. 'I was right,' he said. 'You *are* one good dog.'

★ ★ ★

Fifteen minutes later, they had returned to the stream. Here the fire had progressed slowly because the woods petered out into stony ground. But further north things became much worse. Driven on by the crosswinds that the fire itself had created, the blaze seemed to have looped back on itself, sweeping in a wide arc towards the ridge.

With smoke everywhere, it was difficult for Rascal to get his bearings. Charred, limbless trees stood where there had once been healthy forest. Mike was trying to cut back towards the stream, but Rascal realised that they were close to the place where he had heard a faint cry earlier, right before the din of the helicopter had drowned it out.

Trusting his instincts, he struck out towards the same place now. Mike

hesitated for a moment and then
followed the dog. Soon, though, they
were facing an impenetrable wall of fire.
It seemed to Rascal that flames were

everywhere now. How could they find anyone in this?

But then Rascal heard another thin cry from up ahead, on the other side of the flames. There *was* someone there. The firefighter had heard it too, but he was grimacing as he stared at the scene that faced them.

'No way through,' he muttered.

The fire had curled back on itself, following the natural contours of the land, which dipped down like a bowl. Anyone on the other side of the wall of flame in front of them – Hailey's father or anyone else – was trapped inside a ring of fire. There was no way of getting in there and no way of getting hoses or other equipment this deep into the forest. Even if they could have done so, there would be no time.

Mike, who had tied a bandanna across his mouth as protection against the smoke, seemed unsure of what to do. Rascal too looked around in despair. But then there was a loud crash. The fire at ground level had reached the trunk of a dead oak. Already diseased and dry as an old bone, the wood had burned fast and now the tree toppled forwards with a terrible crash. It fell against the lower branch of a pine that the flames had not yet reached, so that the trunk of the dead oak lay at an angle.

It was their only chance. Until the flames began to consume the rest of the oak's trunk, it made a kind of bridge across the wall of fire.

They could not hesitate. In a few seconds the bridge would be gone. Rascal bounded forwards – 'Hey!' cried Mike – past the flames that fed at the base of the fallen tree, and jumped up on to the wide trunk. He ran along it as quickly as he dared, trying not to look at the flames that danced and roared on

either side beneath him.

In the boiling blackness of the smoke, he had no way of knowing what lay ahead. There was nothing he could do but launch himself forwards into the darkness and hope that he was not leaping into the very heart of the inferno.

The impact jolted him as he hit the earth, but he was unharmed. Seconds later Mike joined him, going into a roll as he landed on the scorched ground.

'Hope you know what you're getting us into, dog,' he grimaced.

They were inside the ring of fire now.

It was almost impossible to breathe, impossible to see anything. Rascal's eyes were bleary from the smoke and heat, but then he caught a glimpse of something up ahead, a flash of purple in the middle of all the black and red and orange. Hailey's dad had been wearing a purple T-shirt — it had to be him! Rascal raced forwards and Mike followed.

The man had taken shelter in a rocky clearing. With fire on all sides, it was plain that this area would not provide safe refuge for much longer. Soon the flames would sweep through the tall, dried-out grass that grew between the rocks. Hailey's father was slumped, his head dropping forwards as he stared at the ground.

When he heard the dog and the firefighter, he looked up and scrambled to his feet. His voice sounded cracked by the heat.

'My daughter!' he began. 'Have you seen her? She's only just six years old, she —'

Mike cut him off. 'She's fine,' he said. 'She's safe, the rest of your family too.' He had taken the backpack off and pulled out a water canister, which he pushed towards the other man. 'It's *us*

we've got to worry about now,' he added quietly.

Hailey's dad wiped water from the side of his mouth with a grimy forearm. 'Where are the others?' he asked. 'Your colleagues?'

Mike gave a grim smile. 'No others out this way,' he said. 'Just us.'

'But . . .' Hailey's father's voice trailed off as he took in Mike's words.

As they looked around, it seemed hopeless. There were no gaps in the wall of fire all around them. The heat was so intense now, they wouldn't be able to last much longer. Even before the fire reached them, it seemed likely that they would run out of oxygen.

Mike was pulling something out of a large plastic pouch he had taken from his backpack. He opened it up and unfolded what looked like a big, heavy sheet of aluminium foil. Reflections of the flames danced on its silver surface.

'This is our only chance,' he gasped, shaking the folds out of the fire shelter. 'But it'll be a tight squeeze!'

With Hailey's dad and Rascal right

behind him, Mike stood with his feet on the bottom corners of the foil shelter. He grabbed the top corners and stretched it up and over them. Then, under Mike's directions, they eased forwards, so that they were lying on the ground, all wrapped up. Rascal couldn't help remembering those potatoes baking in their tinfoil back at the campfire!

The firefighter made sure that their faces were pressed close to the ground where the air was slightly cooler. But it was still so hot in there, it was almost unbearable. Pressed against the two humans, the only thing that stopped Rascal from struggling to poke his snout out of the silver tent was the thought that it was worse by far outside.

'It's like being in an oven,' gasped Hailey's father.

'Well, there's a good reason why these things have the nickname they do,' the firefighter said.

'What's that?'

'We call 'em "shake and bake" – you shake 'em out and then you bake once you're inside 'em!'

Hailey's dad couldn't hide the tremble in his voice. 'How will we know when the fire reaches us?'

'Don't worry,' came the answer. 'You'll know.'

It arrived just minutes later. The noise became worse than ever, like a hundred jets flying low overhead. Rascal hadn't thought that the inside of the shelter could get any hotter, but it did. The animal part of him was tensed to scramble to his feet and flee, to just get away from this terrible danger. But he knew that, however hot it was inside this shelter, it was much, much worse on the other side of it. He wouldn't last two seconds out there.

The noise went on and on, but eventually it subsided a little.

'Is it over yet, do you think?' asked Hailey's dad nervously.

'Better safe than sorry,' answered Mike. 'I reckon we should just stay here a while longer.'

But then the sounds from outside changed. It was as if something was landing on the outside of the fire shelter.

'Could be the slurry,' commented Mike thoughtfully.

'What's that?'

'Chemical fire retardant,' the firefighter answered. 'Planes fly over and drop it right on to the fire.' He paused a moment. 'Funny though – I didn't hear any engine noise, did you? They usually fly in pretty low.'

Meanwhile the sound outside continued. It had a sort of drumming quality to it now.

It was Rascal who understood what it meant first. He wriggled his way out of the shelter. 'Wait, boy! Stop!' Mike cried, but Rascal was already poking his nose out. It was immediately soaked by cool, heavy, wonderful rain. At last! At last the rain clouds from the east had caught up with him!

Moments later, all three were out of the shelter. Its shiny surface had been dulled and blackened by the fire. There was hissing and smoke all around, but just a few flames on the ground. The rain was beating down the flames in the trees as well. Dead and blackened stumps poked up from the scorched earth all around them.

Rascal barked in relief and joy. Mike

was laughing, too. He held his helmet in one hand and laughed and laughed as the rain poured into his mouth and soaked him to the skin. Hailey's dad simply gazed up at the sky, as if giving thanks to the rain that was pelting down on them.

CHAPTER 9

The scene behind the firefighters' line
was very different when they returned.
The fire was not completely defeated,
but the mood of the place made it clear
that the battle against it was as good as
won. There were many more people

bustling around now – paramedics and police as well as firefighters – and a lot more vehicles. There was even a television news crew there.

Rascal recognised the group being questioned by a police officer. It was the four campers who had refused to give Rascal anything to drink earlier that day (though it now seemed like a long time ago). They looked pale-faced and shaken.

But for Hailey's family, no one else in the world existed but each other. The four of them hugged and cried and laughed all at the same time.

Her dad knelt down in front of Hailey.

'Hailey, my brave girl! My brave, brave girl! How did you do it? How did you get back all by yourself?'

'I didn't, Daddy,' she answered. 'The doggy helped me.'

They both looked at Rascal, who was still standing next to Mike.

'Don't ask me who he is,' said the firefighter with a bemused shrug. 'I just know he's one good dog!' He bent down and ruffled Rascal's fur.

'One thing's for sure,' said Kevin, putting an arm round his sister's shoulders. 'I'll never call you a chicken again, ever.' And that was the closest he'd ever come to an apology.

'Excuse me,' said the TV news reporter, who had just finished interviewing someone from the park authorities. 'We've just heard what happened, everything you've been through. I know this is a difficult time, but would you mind if we do a quick interview? Our viewers would love to hear your story – especially how the dog helped save you.' She glanced at Rascal.

'What's his name anyway?'

'Er . . . we don't know,' said Hailey's dad.

Kevin smiled and whispered something into Hailey's ear. She grinned too.

'He's called Champ!' she said.

'It's short for "World Champion Dog",' added Kevin, 'because he's so brave. Right, Champ?'

Rascal gave another bark of happiness.

The cameraman pulled his head away

from the lens. 'I've got them all in shot,'
he said to the reporter. 'Ready when
you are.'

The TV reporter put on her best TV
smile and pushed a microphone towards
them.

CHAPTER 10

A long way away, a teenage girl
called Catherine was sitting with her
homework spread out on the carpet in
front of the television.

'I don't know how you can work with
that thing on,' her dad called from the

kitchen.

''S easy,' murmured Catherine. She didn't lift her eyes from her Social Studies homework, but she was nodding her head along in time with the music video.

There was the sound of a car pulling into the drive. Moments later, her mum appeared at the doorway. She put her bag down on the floor.

'Has your brother come home yet?'

Catherine nodded. 'He's in the back garden,' she said. 'Same as usual.'

In the last few weeks, her brother had taken to sitting out on their old swingset. Of course, he was much too big for it – neither of them had actually played on the swing for ages; the family just hadn't got round to taking it down. No, Joel just liked to sit out there on his own.

Mum cast a worried look out of the window. Her son had become a

different person. Whereas he had once been bright and friendly, he was now quiet and withdrawn. He had dropped out of basketball and swimming at school, and he never seemed to invite friends over or go round to their houses any more. Did he even care about his friends these days?

She didn't need to ask what had caused the change, of course. It was hard not to blame themselves. If only they'd decided not to take Rascal with them on that wretched holiday. If only they'd put him into kennels for a couple of weeks. It was bad enough that the dog had died in a terrible accident . . . The worst thing was that Joel had been there when it happened. He'd seen it all! If it hadn't been for the dog's bravery, Joel might have died himself in those caves.

Joel's mum went into the kitchen, where her husband was carefully adding spaghetti to a large pan of boiling water.

'What are we going to do about him?' she asked.

Joel's dad shook his head and sighed. 'I just don't know.' They'd had this conversation too many times before and he was all out of answers. A few weeks ago they had discussed the possibility of getting Joel a new puppy, one that wasn't anything like Rascal. Perhaps that would take Joel's mind off his lost dog, they had thought. But Joel had shown no interest in the idea at all. He'd just explained, in that new, distant way of his, that no other dog could ever replace Rascal. And then he'd taken himself off to his room, alone again. Somehow that was even worse than if he'd become angry or upset.

Suddenly there was an excited shriek from the living room. 'Mum! Dad! Come quick!'

Both parents rushed into the room.

Catherine was still sitting cross-legged on the floor, but the homework spread before her was completely forgotten. She was staring intently at the television, a look of disbelief on her face.

The music programme had ended and now there was a news round-up on. The screen was filled with footage of a forest fire. A voice was saying, 'According to park authorities, the fire was probably started by a carelessly dropped cigarette. Firefighters battled the blaze with a backfire and finally, with a little assistance from Mother Nature and some much-needed rain, they were able to get the blaze under control . . .'

Dad wasn't exactly surprised at this news story. It had been a long, dry summer and there had been fires in forests and national parks across the country. But why was Catherine so worked up about it?

'Just get Joel! Quick! There's something he *has* to see,' gasped Catherine urgently.

Mum ran to the sliding door and called Joel in from the garden.

The boy slid off the swing and ambled back to the house. Joel never seemed to rush for anything these days. When he got there, the rest of his family was transfixed by the television.

'Yeah?' Joel asked wearily from the door.

But then his eyes fell on the TV too. He only just saw the end of the news item. The reporter was saying, '. . . as firefighters stamp out what remains of the fire, one family here is saying a special thank you to a dog called Champion!'

The picture cut to a shot of a young girl. Her face was dirty with ash and streaked with tears and she was hugging a black and white dog round the neck.

With his tongue hanging out and his bright eyes sparkling, the dog almost appeared to be laughing.

But the dog on the screen wasn't called Champion! Joel would know that face anywhere. He had pictured it in his mind every single day since the accident had happened. There was no mistaking it!

The boy's mouth spread into an enormous grin for the first time in ages.

It was Rascal! He was alive.

Rascal was alive!

Rascal is getting closer to his home, and Joel, but what will his next adventure be? Find out in this special extract from

SWEPT BENEATH THE WATERS ...

CHAPTER 1

Rascal came to the river in the grey
light of early morning.

He'd been on the move since before
sunrise and he had made good time.
But what now? To continue his journey
west, he had to cross to the other side.

The river wasn't too wide, but its level was high after several days of rain and its waters ran fast. A feeling of uneasiness clutched at the dog. Could he swim in such a strong current?

Rascal didn't want to find out. A shiver of fear ran through him at the very thought. He looked up and down the river. One direction led off to nothing but wilderness. In the other, he could make out electricity pylons in the distance. That meant a town. Usually Rascal tried to avoid towns as much as possible – it was safer that way – but he knew there was a better chance of finding a bridge in that direction. He began to follow the river downstream.

The trees around him had started to lose their leaves. A memory stirred in Rascal's mind of playing with Joel in the back garden. He had been no more than a puppy then. Joel had promised his parents that he would rake up the leaves that littered the lawn. And he had made good on that promise, until . . .

'Check this out, Rascal!' Joel had said with a grin. And then he had scooped up a handful of the leaves and tossed them into the air.

'It's raining leaves!' Joel had laughed,

and Rascal had been happy to join
in the fun, jumping up and barking
excitedly.

'What are you two up to out there?'
had come the cry from the kitchen
window. But, as boy and dog rolled in
the leaf pile, Joel had been laughing too
hard even to answer his mum.

But Joel was far away now and the

falling leaves filled the dog with anxiety. Autumn was here. He could feel it on the wind, like a promise of the winter to come. What if he hadn't made it home before the really bad weather set in? He would never be able to continue his journey once the first snows had fallen.

And then what?

The river curved round, and beyond the bend a small road ran alongside it. Rascal was able to pick up speed now, running in the middle of the road but always keeping the river in sight. He didn't even notice the sound of an engine behind him until the blare of

a horn startled him. It was loud and it
didn't sound like car horns usually did.
This one played a few notes of music.

Rascal leapt to the side of the road
just in time before a battered red pickup
truck roared by. The man in the driver's
seat shouted something through the
open window. Rascal watched until the
truck disappeared round the bend ahead.

He continued more carefully now. Soon he passed a few warehouses by the water's edge. And then the land opened up in front of him. He had come to a small park that sloped up from the river. At the far end of the park lay a small town . . . and also a footbridge across the river.

He would be able to cross here.

As he set off in the direction of the bridge, Rascal became aware of the one vehicle parked at the top of the hill alongside the park. It was the red pickup truck, the same one that had passed him on the road earlier. But where was the driver now?

The answer came moments later when a burly man burst out from behind the park's wooden shelter, down near the waterfront. He was in his mid-twenties, with hair cropped close to his head. His face was set in a grimace, as if he wanted to get out of this place as fast as possible.

Over the past few months, Rascal had learned to read humans. It was a matter of survival. With some you could sense their kindness – it almost shone from them like a light. But there were other people Rascal now knew he had to avoid. It had been a hard lesson to learn.

Such people cared nothing about a stray dog like him. If he tried to beg a bite to eat from one of them, he was more likely to receive a snarled insult or even a kick for his troubles.

Rascal was sure of one thing: this man belonged to the second kind. And for the man to get back to his truck at the top of the hill, he would have to go right by Rascal. Fear stabbed at the dog.

Rascal did his best to disappear into himself, to not look up, to act as if he wasn't there at all.

'I can't get away from stinkin' dogs,' snarled the man, when he neared the path Rascal was on. The stale smell of cigarettes was strong on him and . . . something else too, but Rascal couldn't place the scent.

'Beat it!' yelled the man.

Rascal scurried quickly out of range of the boot that lashed his way.

The man ran right past him and up the hill. He pulled open the truck door and soon the engine roared into life. The man revved it a few times and then, with a squeal of wheels on concrete, the truck disappeared down the road.

The dog padded forwards carefully. The man was gone, but Rascal's senses told him that he was not alone in this park. He sniffed the air, finally identifying the scent. He knew it! There was another dog close by, maybe more than one.

But where?

It was only chance that the wind died down at the right moment for Rascal to hear the whimper. It sounded small and frightened, and it came from a line of bushes at the back of the shelter the man had emerged from.

Rascal edged closer. He heard the whimper again, this time joined by another. He pushed his snout through the bushes and saw a canvas bag lying on the other side. An acrid trace of cigarette smell hung around the bag and Rascal knew instantly that the man in the red pickup truck must have left this here.

The top of the bag was open and a tiny snout was poking out.

It was a puppy, a little black-and-brown dog so young that its fur was still fluffy.

Carefully, Rascal nudged the puppy back and then pulled on the opening of the bag. There were two other puppies in there, these ones even tinier than the first. They were snuggling next to each

other for warmth.

Rascal looked around but could see no other dog anywhere . . . no mother. These puppies were all alone.